For Martha
H.W.

To Finnick and Kyle,
*for being my support
and inspiration.*
H.H.

First published in 2016 by Scholastic Children's Books
Euston House, 24 Eversholt Street
London NW1 1DB
a division of Scholastic Ltd
www.scholastic.co.uk
London ~ New York ~ Toronto ~ Sydney ~ Auckland
Mexico City ~ New Delhi ~ Hong Kong

Text copyright © 2016 Holly Webb
Illustrations copyright © 2016 Helen Huang

PB ISBN 978 1407 16516 5

HOLLY WEBB

The Snow Princess

and the

Winter Rescue

illustrated by Helen Huang

SCHOLASTIC

Once upon a time, a little princess lived in a
grand palace, surrounded by glittering winter snow.

The snow had drifted so
deeply that the footmen
had to dig out the great
front door every morning.
Icicles hung from
the palace rooftops, and
the lake was frozen hard.

High up in one of the palace towers,
Princess Amy gazed out at the
sparkling whiteness, and wished
she could run out and
catch a snowflake.

"Pay attention, Amy dear! Try again!" her mother called, and Amy sighed.
She swept a deep curtsey down to the ground, holding out the long skirts of her dress.

Then she looked hopefully at her
mother, and the ladies-in-waiting.

But the Queen shook her head.
"A princess must be graceful.
Like a butterfly!"

The ladies-in-waiting all nodded firmly, twittering,
"Oh yes! Just like a butterfly. Again, again!"
Amy flounced her skirts. Surely the lesson
couldn't go on much longer?

The door swung shut with a tiny click, and Amy held her breath. But her mother and the ladies-in-waiting were still gossiping together.

No one had noticed she'd gone. She was free – no more silly lessons on manners and curtseys and how to stop her crown falling off!

She danced down the stairs and out across the snowy gardens as fast as she could.

Her best friend, Bella, was sliding on the icy paths through the wood.
She called to Amy, "Look, everywhere's frozen!"
Bella caught Amy's hands and pulled her onto the ice, and they
twirled about, slipping and sliding and laughing together.

Amy and Bella slid faster and faster along the icy path. At last they skidded out from between the trees and into a patch of snow-covered reeds at the edge of the river. The two girls sat there in a heap, giggling at their scarlet cheeks and messy dresses.

"Can you hear a noise?" Amy asked. "Something's squeaking." She peered through the reeds and smiled. "A little bird!"

The tiny creature stared back at them, fluttering his soft wings.
The bird was as white as the snow, with dark, jewelled eyes.
"Why doesn't he fly away?" Bella whispered.

"I don't think he can," the princess murmured. The little bird looked
at her sideways with one sparkling eye. Then he hopped onto her
finger, trailing one crisp-feathered wing. "I think his wing is broken.
I'll take him back to the palace until he's better."

Amy and Bella hurried down to the kitchens, with the bird cradled carefully in Amy's hands. Bella's mother was the palace cook, and they begged her for bread, and seeds and the nicest dried fruit she could find.

Then they found a birdcage in the great attics at the top of the palace, and set it out in the princess's bedroom. The little bird sat in the golden cage, and nibbled at the treats, and groomed his injured wing over and over.

The weeks passed, and the white bird grew stronger.

He could flutter about the cage, and hop out onto Princess Amy's shoulder.

He liked to take his food from Amy's fingers, and the princess loved him. She had never had a pet of her own before.

Then one day the white bird stretched out his wings, and flew soaring around the room, twirling through the glittering jewels of the chandelier and crowing in delight. Bella and Amy clapped their hands and laughed as he swooped over their heads.

The white bird began to fly for longer every day. But when he landed, he would perch on the window sill and gaze out at the snow.

Amy fed him the nicest food, from her own plate, but he turned his head away and drooped. "My little white bird is ill…" the princess told her father anxiously, but the king smiled at his daughter, and shook his head. "No. He wants to be free."

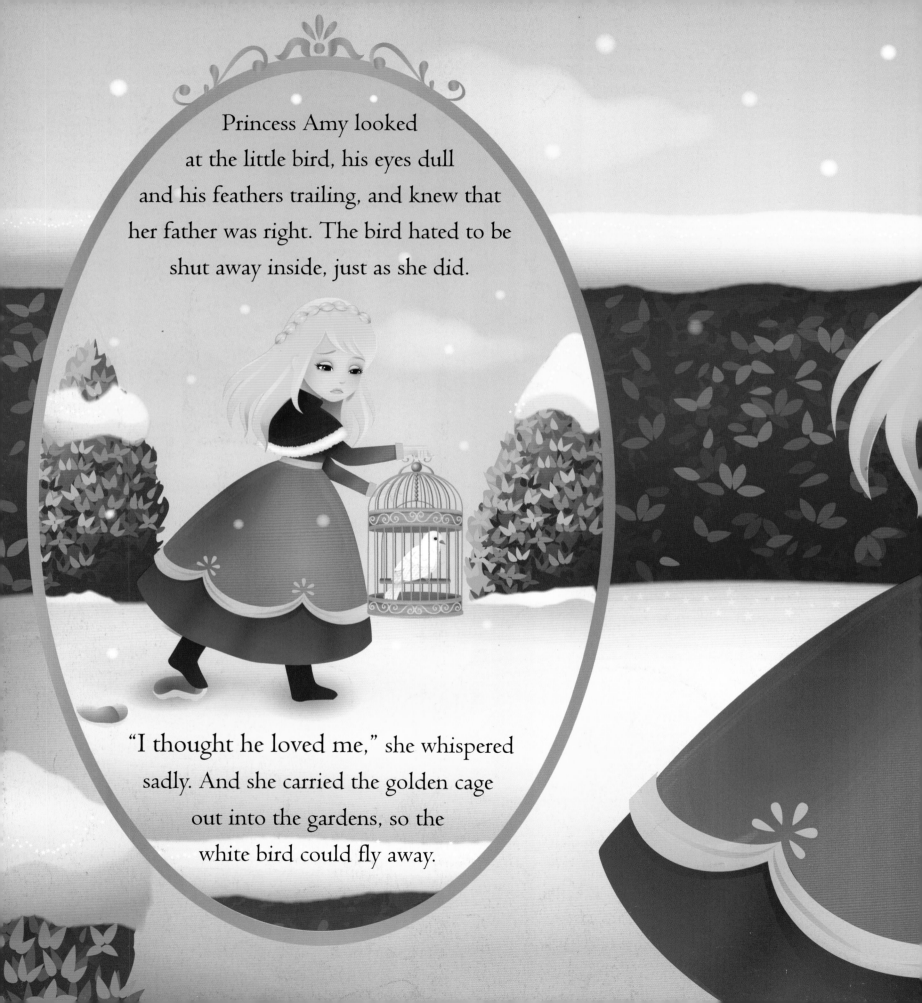

Princess Amy looked
at the little bird, his eyes dull
and his feathers trailing, and knew that
her father was right. The bird hated to be
shut away inside, just as she did.

"I thought he loved me," she whispered
sadly. And she carried the golden cage
out into the gardens, so the
white bird could fly away.

The bird soared into the great sparkling
whiteness, calling out a ringing song of joy.
He flew away, faster and faster, until he
disappeared high in the pale blue sky.
Amy stood watching,
straining her eyes to see.

Then she sat down in a heap on the stone terrace, and gazed at the empty golden cage. "He's gone," she sobbed, and her father swept her up in his arms, and held her tight.

"Won't you come sliding?" Bella coaxed the next day, holding out her hands to the princess. But Amy only shook her head and sighed. She didn't want to play in the woods. She didn't want to play at all. She looked up at the clear blue of the winter sky, trying not to let her tears fall.

Then Amy gasped and stretched
up her hands to the tiny dark speck
spiralling down towards her.

"Little bird, you came back to me," she cried. "I never thought you would."

She smiled so happily at Bella, and the two girls stood together, watching as the snow began to fall. The white bird darted between the snowflakes, and Amy laughed.

"He'll always come back," she whispered, as she went dancing through the snow with her two best friends.